Numby the Numbat

Tales from Tim Faulkner

Illustrated by **Elin Matilda**

Australian GEOGRAPHIC

Numby lived in the woods with his Mum and his Dad,
but he'd grown up so fast that it made them quite sad.
It was time to leave the home he'd outgrown
and find somewhere new, all on his own.

Numby needed to find just the right place,
a new patch of red dirt filled with termites to chase.
He was scared and excited, with his swag on his arm,
and promised his parents, **"I'll come to no harm!"**

Numby ran and ran, like numbats do best,
but no matter where he went, there was nowhere to rest.
He looked to his left, he looked to his right,
and yelled with a gasp as he got a big fright,
because there in front of Numby was a cow!

The cow was in a paddock where the woods had been cleared.
It was so different to home, Numby was more lost than he'd feared.
The cow mooed loudly, **"You don't belong in this place."**
Numby told her he was lost, with a very sad face.

She pointed to the side and said, **"Go this way and you will
find the woodlands you're looking for just over that hill."**
Numby's ears pointed up and his frown levelled out,
he called, **"Thank you, brown cow"** as he ran off with a shout.

Numby ran and ran, like numbats do best,
but no matter where he went, there was nowhere to rest.
He looked to his left, he looked to his right,
and yelled with a gasp as he got a big fright,
because there in front of Numby was a road!

The cars were noisy, bellowing plumes of black smoke.
They frightened Numby so much, he thought he would choke.
They came from one side and went zooming right past,
nearly running Numby over, they were going so fast.

Big trucks, cars and roads he had never seen,
in the forest everything is so natural and clean.
He darted forward and back and from side to side,
and made it across with one last big slide.

Numby ran and ran, like numbats do best
but no matter where he went, there was nowhere to rest.
He looked to his left, he looked to his right,
and yelled with a gasp as he got a big fright,
because there in front of Numby was a fox!

Numby had learnt about foxes in school.
From foreign lands, they were said to be cruel.
Mr Fox was red, and had big, round, green eyes.
He said **"Hello"** with a grin, much to Numby's surprise.

The fox licked his lips and said, **"Please come with me,
I'll take you home and have you for tea."**
Numby jumped up and ran as quick as he could,
taking off in the direction of his dearly loved wood.

Numby ran and ran, like numbats do best
but no matter where he went, there was nowhere to rest.
He looked to his left, he looked to his right,
and yelled with a gasp as he got a big fright,
because there in front of Numby was a person!

Numby was exhausted and stood still for a beat.
Just who was this creature who stood on only two feet?
He was ready to run but as he sped off,
this person said, **"G'day"** in a voice gentle and soft.

Her name was Olive, she was a wildlife ranger,
and she was certain she could rescue Numby from danger.
Numby climbed in, and Olive started the car.
"We're here," she cheered, before they'd gone very far.

Numby ran and ran, like numbats do best.
Now everywhere he went was perfect for his nest!
He looked to his left, he looked to his right,
and yelled with a gasp as he got a big fright,
because there in front of Numby was a numbat!

Her name was Lizzie and he was over the moon,
he'd made such a lovely friend and so very soon!
Little Lizzie told him she'd been all alone
since she'd left her parents, too big for their home.
Numby said, **"Wow, it's the same for me,"**
and they slapped paws and laughed and jumped high with glee.

These new woods they roamed had everything right:
termites, hollow logs and familiar sounds at night.
Numby and Lizzie became really good mates,
and before too long they were going on dates.

One day soon after, on a big hollow log,
Numby shouted to Lizzie, **"Look here, there's a frog!"**
He was playing a trick, what he wanted was a kiss,
that and a cuddle would be pure bliss!

When she turned around, Numby kissed Lizzie,
and they liked it so much that it made them both dizzy.
In the years that came, they had babies of their own,
and helped their species survive in their new woodland home.

Numbat

Other names: Banded anteater, marsupial anteater, walpurti
Status: Endangered

Location

They are normally found in a small part of Western Australian, but are also located in a few fenced reserves in small parts of South Australia and New South Wales.

Appearance

They are small marsupials weighing up to 700 grams. They measure between 35 and 45 centimetres long, and have a bushy tail about the same length as their body. They are usually grey and reddish-brown and have lots of white stripes across their back. They have a long and sticky tongue that they use to find termites.

Saving the numbats

There are less than 1,000 numbats left in the wild. A program known as Project Numbat has helped save the numbat from extinction by raising awareness and funding conservation projects.

Habitat

They are found in areas where there are lots of eucalyptus trees. Their habitat in Western Australia, in particular, is populated with lots of wandoo trees, a medium-sized species of eucalyptus.

Diet

Numbats feed on termites. An adult needs up to 20,000 termites a day, and spends most of its time searching for them.

Shelter

Numbats make nests in hollow trees or logs, filling them with grass, leaves, flowers and shredded bark.

Life cycle

Numbats produce about 4 young a year. Unlike other marsupials, numbats have no pouch to carry their babies. Babies attach themselves to their mother's teats, where milk is produced, and stay there for 6–7 months. They are then left in the nest, or carried on their mother's back. Once fully grown, they are left to hunt and feed for themselves.

State emblem

The numbat is the animal emblem of Western Australia.

Good senses

Numbats have a great sense of smell. This helps them to hunt out termite mounds and nests that are buried just below the ground. They've also been heard to make hissing and tutting sounds when defending themselves.

Predators

Known predators of numbats include carpet pythons, introduced red foxes, and large birds such as falcons, hawks and eagles.

Tim Faulkner

Wrestling a saltwater crocodile, wrangling a deadly taipan and milking a funnel-web spider is all in a days work for Tim Faulkner! He could do all that and still find time to release a blue-tongue lizard, tag a wild platypus and save the Tasmanian devil from extinction!

Tim is a Director and Head of Conservation at the Australian Reptile Park in Somersby, NSWn and The Devil Ark at Barrington Tops, NSW. Australian Geographic Conservationist of the Year (2015), Tim features in numerous TV shows, including his own **Wild Life of Tim Faulkner**, showcasing Australian wildlife to the world.

Tim developed a love for the Australian bush and wildlife at a young age. He is proud to be sharing these stories with children, with the hope they will feel the same love for native creatures. His two sons, Billy and Matty, are particularly happy with the bit where the numbats kiss.

Numby the Numbat

First edition published by Australian Geographic in 2016
An imprint of Bauer Media Ltd
54 Park Street, Sydney, NSW 2000
Telephone +61 2 9263 9813
Email editorial@ausgeo.com.au
www.ausgeo.com.au

Australian Geographic customer service
1300 555 176 from within Australia (local call rate)
+61 2 8667 5295 from outside Australia

Author: Tim Faulkner
Illustrator: Elin Matilda
Art director: Mike Ellott
Designer: Mike Rossi
Editor: Lauren Smith
Sub-editor: Amy Russell
Proofreader: Natsumi Penberthy

Publisher, Specialist Division: Cornelia Schulze
Publisher: Jo Runciman
Australian Geographic editor-in-chief: Chrissie Goldrick
Australian Geographic editor: John Pickrell

Funds from the sale of this book go to support the Australian Geographic Society,
a not-for-profit organisation dedicated to sponsoring conservation,
scientific research, adventures and expeditions.